Je Suis Prest

Foreword

This is the fifth volume of Outlander inspired poetry which I have penned. What started out as being a one- off effort, to raise money for my chosen charity Riding for the Disabled, has become a series.

I am mindful that series 6 of the Starz series is in production and have tried not to stray onto territory which has not been covered thus far by series 1 – 5. I have no idea what the production team have included in the long-awaited series 6, and I am not party to the contents of the 9th Book 'Bees'.

I promised that I would keep writing for your entertainment until the release of 'Go Tell the Bees that I am Gone' or the release of Series 6, whichever came first.

I have chosen to call the book Je Suis Prest - the motto of Clan Fraser. It also means I am ready – and we are all ready and waiting for the next chapters both Televised and written of our favourite series, indeed our obsession.

This book is not compiled in any particular order, the poems are included in the order in which I wrote them, dipping in and out of the books and the series as I went. Some are based on scenes in the books and others on the TV show. They are purely my take on things, sometimes with a tinge of sadness, or joy, or humour or just plain smut and innuendo – but I have tried to keep it clean for any youngsters who may pick this book up.

This is not an official Outlander product, and it is written with a touch of parody and also as a tribute to the works of Diana Gabaldon, her characters, and the actors who portray them.

Any revenue generated from the sale of this book is donated to the charity Riding for the Disabled a charity which provides therapy for individuals with a range of life limiting conditions. I work as a volunteer with this charity and see the amazing work which it does.

RDA It's what you can do that counts

Riding for the Disabled Association
Incorporating Carriage Driving

Acknowledgements

Firstly, to Diana Gabaldon for writing the novels and creating such magnificent characters. These have become an inspiration to many people and have developed a massive fan base Worldwide.

To all those involved in the production of the Outlander TV series which have also generated a loyal and sometimes completely different fanbase, the eternal comparison between book and show will no doubt go on.

To the members of the Facebook Outlander Fan Groups of which I am a member. You have given me so much support and encouragement, indeed some of you have become friends outside of social media. You have provided guidance on spelling, punctuation and grammar, content, and quality all of which is taken on board.

My ever, patient husband who puts up with me disappearing into 'Outlander Mode' every now and again.

My daughter Megan who is my pride and joy and is puzzled that her ancient mother has taken to writing at this late stage.

Contents

Domestic Update

It must be daytime somewhere,
But it's 5am in Wales,
I'm wide awake and thinking,
Of Grand Da telling tales.

I'm trying to type quietly,
Thoughts running through my head,
Listening to the snoring,
From next to me in bed.

I have RDA today,
My husband thinks it's funny,
They've planned an Easter Egg hunt,
And I'm the Easter Bunny.

There's no reply from Scotland,
My kids have run away!
If someone finds them, send them back.
First Class – I will pay.

I've sent some to the Palace,
To our patron Princess Anne,
A Birthday present for the Queen?
They're just the ticket Ma'am.

She has a big one coming up,
She's 95 this year,
Same day as myself you know,
Both, Taurean here.

I'm refreshing from the novels,
To find who's in the mix,
I'm starting with the Christies.
Roll on season six.

The World of Davy Beaton

The door creaked on its hinges,
Was this to be my world,
Bottles named in Latin,
A new career unfurled,

A dungeon full of cobwebs,
It needed a good clean,
What on earth are Slatters,
And what does Purles Ovis mean.

The world of Davy Beaton,
Welcomes me inside,
At least he kept a ledger,
Of all the cures he tried.

Mouse Ears – yes you heard it here.
Is exactly that,
How then do we catch the mice?
I hope I get a cat.

Horse Dung – for a headache,
Is that much of a cure.
And powdered skull of human,
Well, that headaches gone for sure!

Oh hell – slatters they are wood lice!
The bottle hits the floor,
Purles Ovis – well that's sheep shit,
That can kill – I know for sure!

Calum looks implacable,
When I ask about the healer
What about the patients,
I put out another feeler,

Calum's eyebrow raised a touch,
I could have laughed or cried,
When he smiled and told me frankly,
Most of Davy's patients died!

Malva

Curious, intelligent,
A willingness to learn,
But does she have a caring side,
That is a concern?

Brought up by her father,
A strict, religious man,
Kicking at the traces,
Does she have a plan?

Claire has taken her to heart,
Is this a mistake,
Will our heroine survive?
The trouble this girl makes.

Abused by her brother,
Was she willing? Did he make her?
Malva Christie – troubled soul?
Or just a troublemaker!

Conversation at Dinner

Lord Lovat is an old man,
He has an old man's ills,
Intolerant of everything,
Of potions and of pills,

He will not drink much fluid,
I ask him what's amiss,
Bluntly and with no spare words,
He says he can'nae piss.

Told I am a wise one,
He asks my diagnosis,
It's a case of prostatitis.
And what is the prognosis!

Insert a rod into your cock,
To relieve the pressure,
Or massage your internal gland,
Well, that should give you pleasure!

The Old Fox smiled politely,
And declined Jamie's assistance,
My husband's fingers, up his arse,
Would meet with great resistance!

To reduce the pressure,
Would'na cause him too much grief,
He'd let my English digits.
Give him some relief!

Lord Lovat is a devious man,
A fact you cannot miss,
With luck the bastard will explode,
In a shower of blood and piss!

A Clansman at Culloden

I am not a man at arms,
I am not trained to fight,
I follow where my Laird has called,
For Scotland and our right.

Edinburgh was taken,
The British left our City,
Morale was high, we could not lose,
But Battle's never pretty,

We won the day at Preston Pans,
The fog was all around,
Crept round the marsh and woke them up,
Beat the Red Coats sound.

We marched on into England,
But there was no support,
No food, no pay, some drift away,
They will nae fight for naught.

Endless marching, back we turn,
Retreating to our land,
There is no will, to change the Crown,
It's not how Tearlach planned.

Carlisle, Falkirk, Inverness
We take on the way back,
But the British Army
Is clearly on our track.

Exhausted, Freezing, Starving,
There's naught to eat save grass,
We've worn out boots, on worn out feet,
Kilts hanging off our arse,

This Bonnie Prince relies on God,
But the Lord will not provide,
A meagre bowl of Porridge,
To line a man's inside.

The British have their Cannon,
Mustered at Culloden,
And Battalion fire of muskets,
While We are starved and sodden.

~ 17 ~

We can'nae turn and run away.
We will fight, and most will die,
Culloden is the graveyard,
Where a way of life will lie.

Boys will be Boys.

Boys will be boys, they like a prank,
When better than on Sunday,
Cause chaos for the preacher,
Make a much more fun day.

All the Ridge turned out to hear,
Roger Macs first preaching,
Even some of Catholic faith,
Turned out to hear his teaching.

They thought it went unnoticed,
When they let the serpent out,
A brightly coloured king snake,
With a red and yellow snout.

Himself was sweating, nervous,
Standing with his wife,
Him and snakes have history,
Since one nearly took his life.

It's slithering towards him,
Underneath the people's feet,
Twill cause, some consternation,
If it climbs up on a seat,

The sweating warrior draws a breath,
Hopes his nerve won't fail,
He stuffs it swiftly down his plaid,
A good grip on its tail.

The snake is wriggling wildly,
Trying to escape,
Its head pops out above his shirt,
It tries to make a break,

Our hero is now ashen,
But trying to keep calm.
Composure sure is difficult,
With a snake wrapped round your arm,

Cool, calm, and collected,
Claire will take control,
She stuffs it in her pocket,
Before it can reach its goal,

A crisis is averted,
And the sinners will repent,
Roger Mac will see to that.
He saw the whole event.

A long trip home.

A journey tinged with sadness,
To bring my kinsman home,
Fortuitous in one respect,
We travelled all as one.

I promised I'd get Ian back,
At last, to see his ma.
A boy when last she saw him,
Now a full-grown man.

A Lallybroch of sickness,
All the family there,
A sister worn with worry,
Her face showed her despair.

She begged that Claire should heal him,
Demands she speak in tongues.
Claire cannot cure consumption,
And the burning in his lungs.

Ian Mor, his end is near,
He gathers family round,
Giving last words of advice,
no comfort can be found.

We walk upon the hillside,
Talk of times gone by,
He agrees to keep my finger,
'til, I join it by and by.

His whispered words into my ear,
His last to me in life,
He gave me back my sister,
She who was his wife.

He swore he'd always be there,
As sure a dark turns light,
His spirit at my weaker side,
Always on my right.

He will not rest in purgatory,
He lived a better life,
His soul is not so blackened,
As the brother of his wife.

Jenny will leave Lallybroch,
I will take her back with me,
And Ian's light will keep us safe,
In our journey cross the sea.

Frank does his homework.

Do I believe a word she said?
I'm not sure that I do,
Why would she play me false, like this?
If none of it was true?

I thought we had a future,
After the trials of war,
To build ourselves a family,
She's soured that for sure,

I've obsessed about his story,
I've researched back through time,
I've found him in the records,
Is curiosity a crime?

I cannot say I've found her too.
And know she will return,
Drawn like a moth, to candle flame,
To the man who makes her burn.

I must prepare my daughter,
For she will take great pains
Searching for the fiery Scot
Whose blood flows in her veins.

I love my women desperately,
But I cannot live a life,
When he's waiting in the background
To reclaim his wife,

There is, not a day goes by,
She does not drift away,
Across the void of centuries,
Her thoughts are far away,

They will be reunited,
My research tells me so,
The pull of time will be too strong,
And both of them will go.

Diplomacy

All Mackenzie men at arms
Gathered in that hall,
To their Laird, to swear an oath.
To answer if he called.

A gathering, emotive,
Your loyalty you bring,
Tribal and inspiring,
The Clan the only thing.

He tried hard not to be there.
Not to take the stage.
A candidate to lead the Clan,
Til Hamish is of age.

My selfish, feeble, plan to leave,
Would put his life in danger,
He knew I would be captured,
And risked all for a stranger!

A sense of the dramatic,
Playing to the crowd,
He stood before his uncles,
Tall and Fraser proud.

I swear no oath, his words began.
I heard swords start to draw,
If he didn't talk them out of it,
His blood would stain the floor.

A diplomatic masterpiece
Weaved a calming spell.
Appeasing Laird and Clansmen all,
And Dougal knew it well.

Without his great integrity,
Chivalry and honour,
And educated humour,
He would have been a goner.

A Warped Mind

Who knows the depths a mind can plumb?
When it comes to schemes,
This child I'd taken to my trust,
Had schemed beyond my dreams.

A web of lies so complex,
It sounded like the truth,
Complete in minor detail,
Which in her mind was proof.

A bid to take my husband!
To ruin people's lives,
I could feel the gossips,
Sharpening their knives.

Her father – rightly angry,
Her brother – fit to kill,
Jamie – livid to his core,
Malva - lying – still.

I found her in my garden,
Throat slashed with a knife,
Her babies heart still beating,
I tried hard to save its life.

Only time will find the truth,
Our lives are put on hold,
To serve a warped and twisted mind,
And someone's thirst for gold.

Hat Trick

I've a son, and other kinsmen
On the wrong side of the war,
There's a chance that I may kill them,
Or they will end my life for sure.

As a Colonel in the Rifles,
A fact I can't dismiss,
I'm known to be a marksman,
I can'nae always miss.

General Simon Fraser,
Is sat there on his horse,
Surrounded by his entourage,
Lieutenants all, of course.

I take the shot - it's high and wide,
I'm rather glad of that,
But a very junior officer,
Has surely lost his hat,

In the heat of battle,
The Brigadier is shot.
They call me to his death bed,
As his kinsman and a Scot.

I see the young Lieutenant,
Close by Simons side,
He too is the Generals friend,
His grief he tries to hide.

Three of us related,
Frasers all by blood,
To tell him now, he is my son,
Would not do any good.

With Simon dead I walk away,
I think how close I've come,
For the second time I realise
I've nearly shot my son.

Not in proper uniform,
And an officer at that,
The least that I can do for him,
Is give him my hat.

Bath time.

Sparkling like glitter
Warmed up by the sun,
Water is enticing,
It's a source of lots of fun,

Playful then as otters,
Cares shed along the path,
The men discard their clothing,
For their springtime bath.

The greasy grime of winter
Is scrubbed and washed away,
And flexing muscles warmed by sun,
The boys come out to play.

I'm watching from the bushes,
He knows that I am there,
The voyeur in me watching,
Muscles flexing without care.

Swimming, ducking, diving,
The youngsters scream with joy,
At being thrown from man to man,
Just like a bath time toy.

There are no inhibitions,
In this seething mass of muscle
Wrestling with each other
They relish every tussle,

My skin warmed by the sunshine,
I could watch all day,
The first warm day of springtime
When the boys come out to play.

Gut Shot!

It hit me like a freight train,
A bolt out of the blue,
The world turned in slow motion,
My insides boiled like stew.

Burning, searing, terror,
A red- hot trail of lead,
Have I been shot? My hand feels blood,
My side is turning red,

I heard his cry across the field,
He must have seen me fall,
A howl of desperation,
Caused by one musket ball.

The soldier I was stitching,
Left, lying on the ground.
The suture and the needle,
Left hanging from his wound.

The world is turning slowly,
In and out of focus,
Hot and cold are merged as one,
Unconscious hocus pocus......

Sassenach! No – a Dhia!
Why is she outside!
The Church is where there's safety,
She's hit! – she cannot die!

Where the hell's the surgeon,
Someone, stop the blood,
Stay with me Claire, keep breathing,
Yes – in – and out – is good.

Keep the pressure on the wound,
Help her, someone, now!
I'd heal her with my own two hands,
But God, I don't know how!

General sir, your wanted!
The messenger will yell!
My wife is more important,
Tell Lee to go to hell!

I wrote my resignation.
In blood upon his skin,
General Fraser is no more,
I must attend my kin.

Thank God for Denny's steady hands,
And for the power of prayer,
Laudanum and Roquefort cheese,
And the stubbornness of Claire.

She lives to see another day,
Weak and burned by fever,
My commission is resigned,
For I could never leave her!

Unrepentant

I cannot see this as the end,
I've always found an out,
Irish luck runs in my veins,
Of that I have no doubt.

A morbid fear of drowning,
Strange for one like me,
Captain of a smugglers ship
Who lived a life at sea.

I was not brought up honest,
I've lived my life in sin,
Now I'm paying for it,
My tide is coming in.

Every man I ever robbed,
Every man I maimed,
Every woman that I raped,
Every life I claimed,

Measured now in water,
Life's cloth is wearing thin,
I cannot fight against the tide,
And now it's coming in.

Every penny stolen,
Every cruel deed,
Every soul thrown to the sea,
When there was not a need.

Measured now in inches,
As it rises, should I grin,
Or fight against these shackles,
The tide is coming in.

Every last deception,
Every lie I told,
Every man I led to think,
I was not out for gold.

I feel the water rising,
It's now up to my chin,
God will know my prayers as lies,
And the tide will still come in.

The red haired one forgave me,
Offered me a way,
I tried to use her kindness,
I regret it to this day,

Well, I regret that I was caught,
Regret I met her father,
You will not twice deceive a Scot,
Sure, it gets them in a lather.

I've no more time for thinking,
I cannot breathe – Ifrinn.
Blarney will not help me now,
The tide is nearly in.

I've pissed myself, My bowels void,
I'd rather I'd been hanged,
My tide of life is surely in,
And now it's over ....BANG.

The Family Christie.

The story of the Christie's
Would set your nerves a twitch.
Him a deep religious man.
And married to a witch.

Tom Christie left his family,
He sided 'gainst the King.
They hanged his wife for witchcraft.
Her children watched her swing.

His brother's wife was wicked,
All in the good Lord's name,
So, a brother brought a sister up.
He also brought her shame,

Two children living deep in need,
With no true moral guide
Feral and abandoned.
With nothing left save pride.

Tom Christie knew the truth of it,
And he would take the blame,
To save his son the gibbet,
And save, his daughters name.

'Twas the son that wove the web of lies,
I would find out at the end.
There was some good in Malva,
And she thought of me as friend.

To prostitute, your sister,
To cover up your sin.
Tom said the Lord find them out,
And truth at last would win.

Sworn Vengeance

Greed runs deep in some men,
And some can bear a grudge,
Stubborn as the meanest mule,
Their minds you will not budge.

Rather take, what they believe,
Should have been their due.
To ask, they'd think it 'cap in hand'.
And that would never do.

We had kept watch in snow and rain,
Winter on the ridge,
Could not have been much colder,
If we'd had a fridge.

(What is a Fridge Sassenach?)

Arch had sent his good wife back,
To steal the stash of gold,
Buried underneath the house,
Where the Sow lives with her brood.

Merdina fired the pistol,
Ian saved my life,
An arrow deadly accurate,
Killed Arch Bugs good wife.

You should' na send your woman,
To carry out yer plan.
It's your fault that you lost her,
Don't blame another man.

You'll take away what Ian loves,
And ye'll follow him for years,
Ye'll wait until he finds her,
And then you'll cause him tears,

A bitter man, with half a hand
And only half a life.
Old, and nothing left to lose,
Will he avenge his wife?

The Frenchman's Gold

Gold, with three bright diamonds,
Jocasta showed the ring,
Light of many candles
made the white stones sing!

A diamond for each daughter,
And all of them now gone,
Ye ken I was a mother once,
My heart was not a stone,

Three husbands, and three daughters
All of them now dead,
The Cameron thirst for wealth the cause,
Ye should not be misled.

A daughter shot, for three gold bars.
The youngest of my fold,
Lying with the redcoats
Dead beside the road.

The Frenchman's gold is buried,
It lies in Scottish soil,
We could'na carry all of it,
With a country in turmoil.

Three bars were all we carried,
This fine estate they grew,
But tis a hollow empty thing,
With none to leave it to.

Is that the truth? I asked him,
His whispered voice abjured,
Remember she's McKenzie blood,
Do not believe a word!

Her daughters – yes there's truth in it,
Her husband would nae wait.
He Would'na let her say goodbye,
They left them to their fate.

As for leaving gold behind,
That's not the Cameron way,
She's got it hidden somewhere,
Sure, as night turns into day!

Resurrection

It never pays to go against
the wishes of the dead,
They may come back and haunt ye,
If ye dinna see folk fed.

The body wrapped inside the shroud,
She made it as a bride,
Brought it far from Scotland,
Her body it would hide.

Jaw strapped shut with linen,
Eyes drawn down and closed,
Salt and bread beside her,
Quiet in repose.

Old Hiram was a tightwad,
Purse strings pulled up tight.
He saw no need to celebrate,
To set the spirits right.

'I am the resurrection'!
She opened up her eyes,
Granny Wilson is alive,
There's screaming and surprise.

Sitting in her coffin,
Berating Hiram Crombie
With all the folk around her,
Who think, they've seen a zombie.

Where is the food? where is the drink?
This is not a wake!
And where is my good, jewelled brooch.
That was nae yours to take.

Himself produced the Whisky,
Mrs Bug the food,
It pacified the angry corpse,
Lightened up her mood.

Precious few the minutes,
Before she really died,
At least she went in knowledge,
Of what had been supplied.

She did'na think she'd she the day,
She said with some finality,
When she'd be laid to final rest
With papist hospitality.

Carnal Knowledge

Accept some human comfort,
It may just ease the pain,
Until you venture from the dark
To join with life again.

Tis not your love I'm asking for,
I know your heart is taken,
Your mind is in another place,
If I am not mistaken.

Before you sacrifice yourself,
To live a life in chains,
At least remember how it feels,
I make no other claims.

Use it in the long dark nights,
Draw it to your mind,
Keep some human feeling,
Think of those you leave behind.

It's not unfaithful to her memory,
To keep your soul alive,
The memory of human touch,
May just help you to survive.

I heard the voice of Mary,
Answering my prayer,
As I asked God to find a way
That I could forgive Claire.

Her love is very physical,
She thrives on human touch,
To grieve without that contact,
I would expect too much.

At least they have been honest,
And I did'na lose my life,
Despite his Carnal Knowledge,
I love my errant wife.

Mustard Plastered

If the devil could have cast his net,
He would have caught a shoal,
A full house of Rebel Officers
Who only had one goal,

Enticed by Daniel Morgan
A meeting of the great,
Re- enlistment as a General
Was to be my fate.

I was bound for Philadelphia,
To find my wife, of course.
Til that cheeky bastard Washington,
Commandeered my horse.

Several hours later
I'm making shift to go,
A fiery pain shot up my back,
Ifrinn - it's lumbago.

I've never had a poultice,
Applied with so much heat,
Mustard and fresh horseradish,
A Dhia it burns a treat.

I'm Face down on the children's bed,
Friend Hardman rubbed it in,
I'm sure I felt it's searing heat,
Burning through my skin.

Two nights it took to loosen up,
I'd not live them again,
Limping to the privy,
Half crippled by the pain.

Her daughters walked me to the road,
And saw me safe away,
In a load of cabbages
What a way to spend a day.

I stink of sweat; I smell of veg.
with a mustard plaster dressing.
And she has gone collecting herbs,
In the garden at Kingsessing.

When I find my errant wife,
I will'na take excuses,
She may well find the potting shed,
Has one or two good uses.

On the Mend

Murtagh! Where is the patient?
He isn't in his bed,
There isn't anywhere to hide,
And all his clothes are shed,

Why is the window open?
It's very cold outside,
Don't you wink that eye at me,
Your godson may have died!

What on earth has Ellen's smile,
Got to do with this,
Don't tell me that my husband,
Went outside for a piss.

He climbed out through the window!
And I should not be worried!
Murtagh, are you kidding me,
I'm not surprised he hurried,

Murtagh, are you laughing,
Funny! I think not,
I'm losing all my patience,
With a certain red- haired Scot,

I found him walking down the road,
Alone and blue with cold,
Dressed in someone else's clothes,
If I may be so bold.

A man it seems, determined,
To make his wife a widow,
Has not the sense, God gave him.
And climbs naked out the window.

PB & J

I will not let the kids grow up,
Without tasting peanut butter
Claire declared some weeks ago,
What's that? She heard me mutter.

The table laid for supper,
The family gathered round,
What is this dish she's serving?
No one makes a sound!

She's cut the bread in slices,
And then stuck them back together,
Eating this new -fangled thing
May be heavy weather.

I look around the table,
Folk are eating with their hands,
That's not what I was taught to do,
I'm not sure I understand!

Well in I go, I'd better taste,
This thing that's made of bread,
Ken, I'll stab it with my fork.
Best make sure it's dead.

It tastes like nothing natural,
It wraps around yer teeth,
I could fix my shoes with this,
And what's this underneath?

It's sickly sweet, and sticky,
But I'd much rather honey,
Ye can keep yer peanut butter,
I'll nae be wasting money.

Ye could use it tae seal letters,
Or glue back things that's damaged,
But I will no' be eating,
Another peanut, jelly sandwich!

Refugees

Wagon after wagon,
Each loaded up with life,
A family's goods and chattels,
Topped off with a wife,

Some are pushing hand carts,
Belongings piled high,
The collected things that make up life
Pointing at the sky,

The threat of war, The sense of fear,
The City safe no longer,
Humanity is on the move,
Whose army will prove, stronger?

The old, the young, the weak the strong,
The elderly and frail.
Rest along the dusty road,
Moving slowly up the trail.

They have no destination,
Their future is unknown.
Those with nothing surely die,
Before they find a home.

Like snails, their houses on their backs
A family's whole life,
Furniture and belongings,
And on the top – a wife.

Last Resort.

They'd taken Jane for murder,
This was my last resort,
She'd admitted that she killed him,
Been convicted by the Court.

There were no strings the Greys could pull,
They'd hang her in the morning,
Only one man left to ask,
To help before days dawning.

I knocked the door and waited,
Mother Claire let me inside,
He didn't hesitate to come,
He was straight by my side.

Yes, he asked some questions,
Then he made, a plan,
What should I expect, of him?
He's a criminal, this man.

Does he save a fellow murderer?
The dangle from the noose,
Or does he risk his all for me,
To help me spring her loose.

He certainly has all the skills,
To break her out of jail,
He knows that he would hang, himself,
If this mission fails.

Jane has died by her own hand,
In a pool of her own blood,
I could not save her from this life,
Though I believed I could.

He is sympathy and kindness,
He prays over the dead,
A lock of hair for Fanny,
He trims it from her head.

Time is short, dawn comes soon,
We cannot be caught here,
I've learned a lot about this man,
Who holds his family dear.

Is there a place for Fanny?
In this family too,
I will take her to the Frasers,
They will know what to do.

She's welcomed in with open arms,
There are no questions asked.
Strong Scottish arms look after her.
Fanny safe at last.

Ghosts in the past

I can't say I'm alone here,
I've Jenny and the boy,
And lying in the hillside
The source of all my joy.

Taken from me early
At the prime of life,
My red -haired tall Mackenzie bride.
My soulmate and my wife.

The boy away to study,
He's special, that I ken,
He'll do great things when he is grown.
If he stays alive' 'til then.

And Jenny - she's all Fraser.
A dark one like her da.
She'll no suffer all fools gladly,
That way she's like her ma.

That's done with the living,
I must attend the dead,
tend their final resting place,
The stone that marks their bed.

Ach - Mo gradh, I see you,
Moving down the path
Red hair flying as you run.
Yes, I can hear you laugh!

Is that young Willie with ye?
I can see him too.
Have I died and joined ye?
Is wee Robert there with you?

My legs are weak, I'm falling!
Are you real or but a ghost?
Am I lying in the heather?
With the ones I miss the most.

Arrivals and Departures

Some men make an impact,
Even when they're dead,
Or not dead, as the case may be,
hold on to that thread.

He could not come back quietly,
And he'd never comprehend,
That His wife was now his widow,
And was wedded to his friend.

Barging in at Chestnut Street,
He's come to claim his wife!
One warm embrace then off again
Running for his life.

Eye to eye with William,
Who now twigged he was his son,
And redcoats banging on the door,
What has that Scotsman done?

A stand off on the landing,
Holds a gun on Lord John Grey.
Then they climb out of the window
When will he be back to stay?

And I am left explaining,
Picking up the pieces
Of a William in crisis,
I must include this in my thesis.

So, I am a bastard!
My father is a Scot.
All the things I thought I was,
I now know I am not!

He's a criminal, a traitor,
A Jacobite, a groom.
A filthy stinking papist!
Then William left the room.

Losing all composure
Fraser temper fully loaded,
The young 9th Earl of Ellesmere
Finally exploded.

The lovely house at Chestnut Street
No longer has a door,
The chandelier crystals
Are smashed upon the floor.

The bannisters are broken,
The panelling is trashed,
Exit stage left William!
The cause of the strammash.

And waiting on the doorstep,
Like the perennial bad penny
Quarrels all forgotten now,
Is Jamie's sister Jenny!

She calmly raised an eyebrow,
Willie charged out through the door,
The son is like his father then?
She didn't have to say much more!

Changeling

A tree so dark and ivy green,
Boughs like enfolding arms,
Grows on a hill of moss and fern,
Made strong by fairy charms.

It bids you leave the ailing child,
The wee folk gave to you,
And swap it for the changeling,
If the legends are all true.

The child you leave will be at rest,
And your own is safe and well.
Living with the fairies now
It may come back, who can tell.

Simple folk believe these things,
It helps to ease the pain,
Of grieving for a lost one,
It helps them live again.

To try and heal a changeling child,
Is witchcraft in itself,
Leave the infant to its fate,
As fairy or as elf.

The parents will be watching,
From a hidden place close by,
The child will die, you can'nae help,
No matter how ye try.

Do not reap the anger,
of the ignorant and poor.
Superstition lives in them,
And rules their lives for sure.

They've minds that see no further,
Than church and one good meal
To them you are a Sassenach
And their souls you'll steal.

I warn, ye will not change folk,
Their lives you won't enrich,
They'd rather tie ye to a pyre,
And burn ye for a witch.

Ye ken ye din'nae know their ways.
They will'na hark to reason.
It's entertainment for the mob.
To burn a witch in season.

Shovelling Shit

Spoiled rude and arrogant,
A voice that grates on glass,
We'd love to bring her down to earth
And kick her up the arse.

Fetch my horse, you useless Scut,
I'm going riding now,
Dirt on her shoes she thinks us,
But we serve her anyhow.

Now she's started choosing,
Her escort for her ride,
I'm shovelin' shit milady,
There is nowhere to hide!

Asking if I'm married,
Sure, I know what tae do!
But if you were the last on earth,
I'd not do it with you!

So ye'd send me back to prison,
Blackmail me with threats
Send soldiers into Lallybroch,
You're as low as you can get.

Next, I'm climbing in through windows,
An errand for a fool,
Lest she curtail my freedom,
I'm breaking every rule.

One night she gets, it is not love!
She may not use my name,
But I may just teach her one thing,
That life is not a game.

And now it's nine months later,
And the household in a frenzy,
If anyone adds two and two,
You're in the shit Mackenzie!

Syrup of Figs

It wasn't a big secret,
That Sandringham liked boys,
The prettier the better,
He treats them as his toys.

I was sent to Leoch,
To learn my Ps and Qs
And was just what he fancied,
To play with and abuse.

Twas a game of cat and mouse
He'd hunt me out each day.
Get me in a corner
And his games he'd try and play.,

I kept my wits about me,
Each time he made a pass,
I Would'na turn my back on him,
He'd do more than pinch my arse.

He requested that I wait on him,
His steward taken ill,
He needed help to wash and dress,
He was going for the kill.

I went down to the kitchens,
And asked good Mrs Fitz.
For a dose of her best medicine
Fer when ye can'nae shit.

She gave me one good spoonful,
But That may not hit the spot,
Before I wait on Sandringham
I'll go back and drink the lot.

I made my best excuses,
With a very solemn face.
And went running for the privy,
Before he tried his case.

I hid up in the stables,
Until I could leave town
I had to get to Lallybroch.
Before my breeks turned brown.

Syrup of figs will clear you out,
One dose is all you need,
He who drinks the bottle,
Must run very fast indeed.

Otter Tooth

A skull half buried in the leaves,
An Opal, sparkling bright,
Ghostly footprints through the mud,
The guide that set me right.

Lightning dancing in the trees,
a pole of fire burns
A rearing horse, I hit the ground,
Unconscious in the ferns

Shelter found under a tree,
I emptied out my boots,
Then made a place to lay my head,
Nestled in its roots.

Hard as rock beneath the leaves,
A skull of bleached white bone,
An opal, large to fill your hand,
The brightest coloured stone.

A torchlight waving in the trees,
Not held by mortal hand,
A ghostly silent Indian
Wandered on this land.

A ghoulish wound upon his head,
His skull was cleaved in two,
Twas, clear he had a violent end,
Who was he? I'd no clue.

At dawn I found my boots had gone
Was this ghost a thief,
Then I saw the footprints,
I must follow them, relief.

I tracked them through the woodland,
I walked as in a dream,
To Jamie and the horses,
And my boots beside the stream.

The Indian spirit guided me,
But what I found most chilling,
His teeth had modern dental work,
And several silver fillings.

A sign indeed, he brought us here,
We need no longer roam,
The stream led us to Frasers Ridge,
The place we made our home.

Ulysses

I am more than just a servant,
Answering her call,
More than just the Butler
Standing silent by the wall.

I know the darkest secrets,
This family keeps tight,
I know the grief Jocasta keeps,
Hidden from your sight.

She marries for protection,
Never more for love,
And I will be here by her side,
Black hand in white glove,

I am her eyes, I see for her,
I watch while she holds court,
I would give my life for her,
Without a second thought.

She plans and she manipulates,
She tries to get her way,
When all she wants is family,
And she wants them all to stay.

There is a sadness in her life,
Which can't be cured by gold.
A fear of being left alone,
Blind and growing old.

I will never leave her,
And no - I'm not a slave,
I love the woman desperately,
I'm Ulysses the brave.

A Ghoustidh,

Do not waver!
And he did not
The hunters shot, was true,
It burned through clothing, searing flesh,
It tore a heart in two.

Dinna Fash!
he did not
It does'nae hurt' he said.
Fine words, from a fine brave man
I could nae see him dead.

Help Me!
So, we carried him,
Limp into the tent,
Save him, please, ye have to!
A Ghoistidh, is not spent.

Hold my words?
I did not!
I said what none would dare,
To wage war, for one's own glory,
Was never to be fair!

Duty done!
I've finished,
I'll no more, serve the Crown,
That coat burned on my shoulders,
I threw it on the ground.

Goodbye!
Beloved kinsman,
Guardian of my life,
Your blood is salty with my tears,
my daughters and my wife's

Am I ready!
No, I am not.
Now I face the toughest test,
Murtagh Fitzgibbons Fraser
I must lay your soul to rest.

Peaceful!
I release you,
Lay your soul to sleep,
Your spirit will protect me,
It needs no oath to keep.

Justice!
No, there was none,
For the loyal men that fell,
The musket ball that pierced your heart
Ripped mine apart as well.

A restless night

Heads I win, tails you lose,
I always get the bed,
Ian's coin is loaded,
He sleeps on the floor instead.

Snowbird is a canny chief,
He asks the King for guns,
But his men will kill without them,
When more raiders come.

I was thinking of the feel of home,
And drifting off to sleep,
A strong light hand upon my balls,
Caused my mind to leap,

Hell, there's a woman in my bed,
Ifrinn there may be two,
Nephew – tell them they should go!
I've no words for what to do.

I'm flattered that they honour me,
But I am not the King,
I would nae say I'm well endowed,
Hmmm tis nae small thing!

It's raining hard, they can'nae leave,
Uncle, they must stay,
And they are staying in yer bed,
I think ye'd better pray.

That night I hardly slept a wink,
I'd one hand on my kit
A man's cock has no conscience,
Mine was fighting back a bit!

Lying flat upon my back,
I prayed for some restraint,
An Indian lass on either side,
And a cock stiff in complaint!

Major Macdonald's Wig

Us cats are fussy in our friends,
Independent in our ways,
We come and go just as we like,
It's how we spend our days.

We love to play, we love to hunt,
We can combine the two,
if we can have a bit of fun
That is just what we'll do.

The Major has a curious thing,
It lives upon his head,
It moves sometimes like it's alive,
I'd best make sure it's dead.

I'll stalk it, and I'll pounce on it.
It's really not that big,
Then I'll claw the life from it,
That thing he calls his wig.

I'll wait until he's gone to bed,
And the wig is fast asleep,
Then I'll kill it like a mouse,
Before it makes a squeak.

Get out of here you F'ng cat,
The wig is out of sight,
He picks an item off the floor,
And throws with all his might.

As I dodge the flying boot,
That drives me from his room,
I hear my mistress laughing,
And a door creaks in the gloom.

Safe in the master's bedroom,
I do what nature calls,
forget about Macdonald's wig,
I'd rather lick my balls.

Petty Jealousy

Walk with me, we walked a while,
Twas awkward from the start,
The boy could be his only son,
And from him he must part.

Talk with me, So, we talked of him,
The boy without a mother,
Born to wealth and privilege,
A life which well could smother.

Listen, will ye watch for him,
Bring him up as yours,
Honour and integrity
Oozes from your pores,

Mind him, when he's growing up,
He'll be headstrong, he'll be wild.
Keep from him who his father is,
He'll not know he's, my child.

Then he offered me his body,
Tested with a kiss,
A bargain with his demons,
No, I'd not dishonour this.

I knew he could not love me,
He is not made that way,
We will be friends despite all this,
And friends are what we'll stay.

And so, he gave me Willie,
And I had an excuse,
To keep in touch when needed.
When I feel I am of use.

You do not have to like me Claire,
But he and I are tied,
As surely as he is to you,
And you know I have not lied.

I feel your petty jealousy,
But you have nought to fear,
I know his mind, you have his soul,
He made that very clear.

Consumption

Was it fate that we arrived,
To witness Ian's end,
His youngest son returning,
Along with his best friend.

The family all gathered,
He'd made his peace with life,
He said goodbye to each of them,
But not yet to his wife.

She found me in the barn yard,
She begged me heal her man.
Tell me you can cure him, Claire!
Her desperate words began.

Consumption is an evil
For which there is no cure,
A dreadful bleeding coughing death,
And death it is for sure.

The cough he caught in prison,
Never left his chest.
It ate his flesh, made him weak,
With time he was not blessed.

Then she called me vengeful,
Asked why I did not stay,
For all the hardship suffered
In the time I was away.

I'm a healer, no magician,
She does not understand.
There is no cure, no magic salve,
No potion at my hand.

She begs me for forgiveness,
Tells me of her plan,
To never lose her brother,
She must tie him to the land.

With me he'll always wander,
We have no settled home,
She knows now that we two are one,
He will never let me go.

Her husband is a good man,
Eternally a friend.
I'd cure him if there was a way.
On that she could depend.

I hope that we can make a peace,
And both of us forgive,
Let Ian know that we are friends,
In the time he has to live.

For die he will, and then his soul,
Flies pain free to the light,
But always there on Jenny's left,
And guarding Jamie's right.

After the Bastille

The thing I wouldn't tell him,
But from my face, he knew.
He has acute perception,
Of everything I do.

Laid out in terms of black and white,
A deal to save a life,
Like the one he made for me
When I was first his wife.

It wasn't that I'd done the act,
But that I didn't trust,
That he would see the reason,
I had done what I must.

A complex man, but simple
In many ways I've found,
He sees things clear as right or wrong,
There is no middle ground.

Lying naked in the grass,
We talk of things unjust,
With little blocks of honesty,
We try and rebuild trust.

With mortar made of unsaid words
And grievances unaired,
Reassurance forms a roof,
Our shelter is repaired.

Then there is possession,
Can the occupants move in?
One blood, one bone, one body,
One soul, one love, one skin.

Time will never part us,
Our whole is far too brave,
But for now, we cling together,
Like those two souls in the cave.

All the Kings Horses

The Percheron, a noble beast,
An equine aristocrat,
The Kings fine livestock on display,
And the human sort, at that.

Courtiers in their finery,
Ladies in high fashion
Picnics on the lush green lawns
Discussing equine passion.

Idle chatter is disturbed,
There's mischief in the making,
Commotion in the stables,
Starts the heads a shaking!

Fergus tiny as an ant
Clinging to his mane,
The frightened colt shot down the field,
Its intention plain,

A muttered voice behind me,
A threat or something worse,
I'll surely beat him black and blue.
Or that horse will do it first.

A flash of tartan running,
A figure dressed in plaid,
Drops on Fergus from the tree
He's rescuing the lad.

A mass of leaping tartan
Wraps Fergus like a quilt.
The court of France can see quite clear,
What's worn under the kilt!

Boy and man lie winded,
They won't admit to pain,
That was so much fun Milord,
Can we do it all again!!

The Price of Treason

A man who looked quite sinister,
Standing in our hall,
Why on earth, should this man
Monsieur Forez come to call.

The pretext of a message,
And a package full of herbs,
A description then so graphic
That he quite ran out of verbs!

He listened calm and quizzical,
To a description of the art,
Of a traitor's execution
And removal of the heart.

The partial strangulation
The eyes and tongue protruding
The shirt removed, the entrails too,
And all the while alluding.

The last major incision
And removal of the heart.
The prisoner is still alive!
He gets to see this part.

For Forez goes to England
Where there is rebellion dawning,
He came to tell my husband.
He meant it as a warning.

To play it false with both sides
Is a very dangerous game.
For no matter who the winner is,
The result is just the same.

When it comes to changing Kings,
Don't sleep easy in your bed,
For if your double dealings found,
You'll not just lose your head.

Souixante Neuf

He's out again in gay Paris,
Drinking with the Prince,
Rebellion and politics,
The talk amongst the chintz.

Do I trust him in a whorehouse?
I really have no choice,
In gay Paris society,
Women have no voice.

Do I feel neglected?
Bet your life I do,
I feel like throwing crockery,
And screaming like a shrew.

I hear footsteps on the stairs,
The wanderer is nigh,
Judging by the smell of him,
He's drunk Paris dry.

Ah, feeling like that are you?
You've really got a cheek,
To think you'll get a welcome,
I've not seen you for a week.

What's that you're trying to tell me,
You've got your mojo back.
You'll really tell me anything,
To get me in the sack.

Ah, yes, I've heard of sixty-nine.
And yes, it counts as well.
What else did you do with her,
I'm listening – please tell.

So, thought of killing Black, Jack,
Brought your hormones to the fore.
Made you feel a man again.
So, you tried it on a whore!

You won't talk me round, with kisses,
I know you'll tell me lies,
You cannot just explain away,
Teeth marks in your thighs.

Can I find forgiveness,
He's just trying to mend his head,
And I really can't resist him.
Jamie, please come back to bed.

My Daughter's Wedding.

I've only known her lately,
Now I'm giving her away,
My wee girl getting married,
Today her wedding day.

Old the pearls around her neck,
New, whisky from the still
Borrowed, is my time with her,
Blue, the flowers, from the hill.

The groom is waiting, nervous!
He's nearly cut his throat,
I had tae help him shaving,
He's blood all down his coat.

The Frasers of the Ridge are here,
To celebrate this match,
And the Governor and his redcoats,
With politics to hatch.

A Presbyterian service,
No Latin and no Priest,
Ye ken they are all heretics!
But they're married now at least.

With my brown- haired lass beside me
We remember all our vows,
From this day forth, and until death,
Are all that God, allows.

One man sorely missing,
There's no Murtagh at this do,
But the Bride has sixpence from him.
Tucked inside her shoe.

I sense a presence watching,
A spirit from the dead,
Watching from the shadows
Frank will see MY daughter wed.

There's music and there's dancing,
They'll drink until they fall,
You can rely on Lord John Grey,
To out drink them all.

With young Jemmy in our care,
It's off to bed we're heading,
Feuds and battles set aside,
At this family wedding.

Jocasta is still scheming,
An heir is still her goal,
As Roger Mac so aptly said,
Cram it up yer hole!

The Call to Arms

He lit the cross, fire at his back,
Red hair gleamed in the flames,
So, Tryon says he wants a Scot,
Let's play him at his games.

A highland figure dressed in plaid,
His voice is ringing out,
Calling all to stand by him,
And all thronged to his shout,

An oath was sworn, stand by his hand,
Though they are not a Clan
Settlers all, in this new land,
They will stand by this man.

A figure framed in leaping fire,
Dirk and sword a glow
Arms spread to call his people close,
To face a common foe,

A Rally cry to all who hear,
Emotive words are spoken,
Eloquent in rhetoric
An oath not to be broken,

Inspiring all to loyalty
A community bound tight
To stand beside its founder
And fight for what is right.

His people see the strength of him,
The steel inside the man,
Forged in the fire of forty-five,
And tempered by this land.

A match made in hell!

His sister begged him marry,
She knew we'd history,
The English whore deserted him,
Now he could marry me.

I saw he bore great sorrow,
He'd lived a rare hard life,
But now I had my chance of him,
He'd take me as his wife.

He craved the life of family,
The bairns he hadn't fathered,
My girls are daughters to him,
But there was one he'd rather.

The witch was at my wedding,
Standing in the Kirk,
Between us at the altar,
Our marriage could not work,

The whore was in my bridal bed,
He called her name out loud,
He felt her hand upon him,
When his member stood up proud,

She cast her spell upon him,
All those years ago,
He was mine before that time,
Pride would not let him go.

Two husbands and two daughters on,
He's a shadow of a man.
But he'll keep me and provide for me,
Send money when he can.

We all thought the Sassenach,
Had died during the war,
But here she is as large as life,
And standing at my door.

He married me from pity,
I treat him now with spite,
He never really needed me,
Especial that night.

And she who charmed him from me,
Still has him in her spell,
English whore, Sassenach witch,
I damn your soul to hell.

Tulach Ard! - A Fireside Story

Working in the woodland,
A new pen for the hogs
Jemmy had escaped his mum,
To help us carry logs,

A hoard of stolen biscuits,
Smeared upon his face,
Smelling sweet with honey
He toddled round the place,

Big Pig! he cried, and there it was,
A boar of massive size,
With tusks as long as Jemmy's arm,
Bloodshot piggy eyes.

It looked at us and grunted,
Then Jemmy screamed in fright,
In a flash the boar had charged,
Into my line of sight,

Roger Mac had dived on it,
To wrestle it away
Then I screamed out Tulach Ard!
Grand da will save the day.

I drew my dirk, I crouched to fight,
I saw it shake its head,
One slip one fall, one careless move,
Grand da would be dead.

Here ye great fat f'er,
I challenged it to fight,
It ran at me with tusks outstretched,
I lunged with all my might.

Then I slipped and dropped the dirk,
I felt a few ribs crack,
A fence post speared it in the side,
The boar still fought us back.

Jemmy stop, ye can'nae help,
He toddled t'wards the beast,
The boar stopped still and licked its chops,
preparing for a feast.

Then came a wolf to join the fray,
Growling fit to burst,
Attacks the boar with gnashing teeth,
I'm glad it got there first.

.

A whistling thump, then silence,
The arrow hit its mark,
An Indian standing silent,
Emerging from the dark.

Wolves and then a Mohawk
And a very big dead hog.
A closer look, brings sure relief,
It's Ian and his dog.

Welcome home! My nephew,
A timely entrance that,
We've bacon for at least a month,
Let's away and chew the fat.

The Garrison Commander

Upstairs in a private room,
The table set for twenty,
Dining on the finest fare,
Food and wine a plenty.

British Army Officers,
Shirts stuffed out with pride,
Disdain is oozing from them,
All Scotsmen are decried,

With overdone good manners,
They bid me join their table,
Tell of my adventures,
Amuse them with my fable.

And Dougal my protector,
Ridiculed and scorned,
Holds his temper firm in check,
While he is suborned.

Taunted and insulted,
Pushed unto the hilt,
To answer that old question
what is worn under the kilt?

That Braying English Nincompoop
Does he wish to die!
Don't push the War chief further!
Please just let it lie!

Call him Chief Mackenzie,
He's your equal, do you hear!
The Lairds appointed war chief,
Has gone to get a beer.

Then enter Black Jack Randall.
Under my breath I curse
He'll ask me awkward questions!
My day can't get much worse!

I Feel your pain.

My fingers know each scar he has,
And he has one or two,
His back laced like a spider's web,
And I've stitched a few,

His long firm lines of muscle,
The bones beneath his skin,
Lie still in sleep, but ready,
The mask he wears is thin.

I touch the hair, I know so well,
His lips curl in a smile,
A peaceful, calm expression
I've not seen for a while.

The hollow of his belly,
With not an ounce of fat,
Muscled chest to rest my head,
And curl in like a cat,

I know that he can feel me,
Through two hundred years
I wish that I could be there,
To help allay his fears,

He calls me when he's fevered,
He calls me when he's ill,
Lonely or in mental pain
He knows I am there still,

We lie on different sides of time,
Each lies with another,
One in a cell with twenty men
Me with my former lover.

He cries my name! I hear his pain!
My senses spring to life,
It breaks my heart that I'm not there,
To live life as his wife.

A small draught horse.

Where did this woman come from?
She is nae like the rest,
She speaks her mind, she's feisty,
And she's sitting on my chest!

She's already fixed ma shoulder,
She knows just what she's doin',
If it was left to Angus,
My arm would be a ruin.

All the way to Leoch,
She's sat between my thighs,
The feelings rather pleasant,
Ken, she doesn't realise!

It's nice and warm wrapped in his plaid,
I feel his body heat,
I won't admit to feeling more,
That would be indiscreet.

But he's very damned attractive,
I could sit like this all day.
Hell, I'm a married woman,
I shouldn't feel this way.

I'll tend his wounds,
My god his back! He's open with his past,
He frankly tells me everything,
From the first stroke to the last.

Who is this boy, who comforts me?
He's got my senses wired,
I feel that underneath his kilt.
He's really not that tired.

Oats for Breakfast!

What a way to start the day,
Only half awake,
A warrior's hands upon my thighs,
I like this – no mistake,

Soft lips have wandered down my skin,
Exploring every nook,
Tongue and teeth are all in play,
I know that blue eyed look,

He lost himself in pleasure,
There's banging on the door,
Don't stop now, ignore it,
Use that tongue some more.

Wake up! We can't be more awake,
Intent on giving pleasure,
After this I'll pay him back
At least in equal measure.

No! He will not be put off,
He's finishing the job,
Murtagh banging on the door,
Will not this pleasure rob.

Are ye worn out Jamie,
From servicing yer wife,
That ye can'nae rise from bed,
Not to save your life.

I groan a bit in pleasure,
And hide beneath the sheet,
Murtagh looks embarrassed,
He has been indiscreet!

Copyright

Thank you
For your support &
Riding For the Disabled
Best Regards

Maggie J

Made in United States
North Haven, CT
09 November 2021